The pitch was high, but Jacob started
his swing. And then he tried to
hold up.

He thought maybe he had.

But he heard the umpire bellow,
"Steee-rike three!"

Jacob sank right to the ground.

He had let the whole team down.

How could the Dodgers lose to the
Reds?

He had been wrong about watching
the game from the bleachers. That
wasn't the worst thing in the world.

This was it. Losing a game for the
whole team.

Jacob wanted to dig a hole under
home plate, climb in, and die.

*Look for these books about the
Angel Park All-Stars*

ANGEL PARK All Stars

6

PRESSURE PLAY

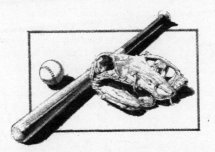

By Dean Hughes

Illustrated by Dennis Lyall

Bullseye Books • **Alfred A. Knopf**
New York

A BULLSEYE BOOK PUBLISHED BY ALFRED A. KNOPF, INC.
Copyright © 1990 by Dean Hughes
Cover art copyright © 1990 by Rick Ormond
Interior illustrations copyright © 1990 by Dennis Lyall
ANGEL PARK ALL-STARS characters copyright © 1989
by Alfred A. Knopf, Inc.

Library of Congress Cataloging-in-Publication Data
Hughes, Dean, 1943–
Pressure play / by Dean Hughes.
p.   cm.—(Angel Park all-stars ; 6)
Summary: When the Angel Park Dodgers get so rattled by the Reds that they can hardly play baseball, rookie Jacob attempts to relax them with meditation exercises he finds in a psychology book.
ISBN 0-679-90431-X (lib. bdg.) : —ISBN 0-679-80431-5 (pbk.) :
[1. Baseball—Fiction.] I. Title. II. Series: Hughes, Dean, 1943–   Angel Park all-stars ; 6.
PZ7.H87312Pr   1990
[Fic]—dc20   90-31307 CIP   AC

RL: 2.6
First Bullseye Books edition: August 1990
Manufactured in the United States of America
1 2 3 4 5 6 7 8 9 10

for Larry McKay

PRESSURE PLAY

★ 1 ★

Off the Team

"This is my day," Jacob Scott said. He took a breath of the warm morning air. "I feel *good*."

Kenny Sandoval laughed, but then he said, "If you hit against the Mariners the way you did at practice last night, you're going to feel even better."

And Harlan Sloan said, "Yeah, what was with you? You made some catches I couldn't believe."

Jacob grinned. He liked hearing this stuff. He really had found his groove. He was hitting clean line drives, and he was fielding better than he ever had.

"The coach even told me I was playing great. Maybe he'll let me start today."

Jacob and Kenny and Harlan were rookies on the Angel Park Dodgers Little League team. They had improved all season. Kenny was one of the best players, and Jacob and Harlan were getting a lot of playing time.

The boys were walking toward the four-diamond complex in their town park. They saw Rodney Bunson, their best player, running toward them.

"Hey, good news!" he yelled. "The Reds just lost to the Padres."

"*All right!*" Jacob said. "That gives them two losses. If we win today, we'll be tied with the Giants for first."

"Hey," Bunson said, "the Giants might lose to the A's. The Giants aren't that hot when Halliday isn't pitching."

Jacob liked that thought. The Dodgers had won the first-half championship without losing a game. Then they started out the second half with a loss to the Reds, and things looked bad. But now the Reds and Giants were having their troubles too.

The Dodgers could still win it all.

"We can't worry about the other teams," Kenny said. "We just gotta get tough and beat the Mariners."

"Don't worry," Jacob said. "We're going to *kill* 'em today."

Jacob had the feeling that nothing could go wrong today.

And then he heard the coach.

"Jacob, I want to talk to you."

Jacob turned around. He saw Coach Wilkens walking along behind, carrying the equipment bag.

This was it.

He was going to ask Jacob to start the game today.

Jacob waited, trying not to grin, but his freckled face left no mistake that he was happy.

"Yeah, Coach?"

But the coach looked serious. He stopped and put down the bag. "I just talked to your dad on the phone," he said. "He's pretty upset with you."

Jacob knew all about that. His teacher had called—again—and said that Jacob was not doing his best work at school.

"Your dad says the only thing you care about anymore is baseball."

Jacob shook his head. "He's just mad because I had some homework one night and I played ball with Kenny and Harlan—and I forgot all about it. So now he puts all the blame on baseball."

"But Jacob, this isn't the first time. I warned you about this two weeks ago—the last time your dad talked to me."

Jacob shrugged.

It was true, of course. But the coach didn't have to make such a big deal out of it. Jacob knew all that stuff they taught at school. He was one of the smartest kids in the third grade.

"Jacob, baseball is fun. But it's not as important as your schoolwork."

Jacob wasn't sure he believed that—since he wanted to be a big-league player someday—but he nodded and said, "I know."

"You're as smart as any kid I've ever coached. You can rattle off baseball facts all day long."

Jacob let his grin come back a little. He was proud of his baseball knowledge.

"But you have to settle down and get serious. Your teacher says you've gotten behind, and it's only because you're goofing off and not doing your work."

"Okay, I'll get caught up, Coach. School will be out for the summer in a couple of weeks anyway, and then I won't have to worry about it." Jacob turned to walk away.

"Jacob, it's not quite that simple. Your dad and I agree on this. You won't play any more until your teacher says you're working the way you should."

"But Coach, I—"

"As of right now, you're off the team. I hope it's not for long, but if you don't start settling down in school, it will be for the rest of the season."

"But . . ."

"No buts, Jacob. You can watch the game from the bleachers if you want, but don't come into the dugout. I'll tell the umpire you're suspended, and we'll play with eleven players."

"Coach, I'll work really hard. Honest. I'll do everything I'm supposed to."

"Jacob, someday you'll thank me—and

your dad—for kicking you in the butt when you needed it."

Adults always said things like that.

But Jacob was in no mood to thank anybody. He had been hitting the ball *so* well. He had *known* this was going to be his day.

Jacob walked slowly to the bleachers. Lots of townspeople were coming to the games now that the Dodgers were doing so well. But he sat near the end—away from everyone.

The Dodgers' players soon spotted him, and they wanted to know what was going on.

Jacob didn't answer. He was fighting back tears.

When warm-ups were over, Kenny ran around the fence and climbed into the bleachers. "What are you doing?" he asked.

"The coach kicked me off the team."

"What?"

Jacob didn't want to talk. He looked away from Kenny's eyes. "Until I do better at school."

"Oh, brother." Kenny put his hands on

his hips and shook his head. "Jacob, he's warned you before. Why didn't you get things caught up?"

Jacob had no answer for that one.

The game was about to start. Kenny had to go back to warm up his arm. He was pitching today.

And so he left, and Jacob sat in the bleachers by himself.

Jacob knew this was the worst day of his life.

And then it got worse!

About half the guys on the Reds' team came wandering along in front of the bleachers and decided to stay and watch some of the Dodgers' game. They picked out some seats just down from Jacob. And one of them noticed him.

"Hey, kid," the boy said, "how come you're up here?"

Jacob looked away.

"Hey, number six, what's the matter?" another guy said. It was Jimmy Gerstein, the smart-mouthed third baseman. "You look like you're going to cry."

Jacob didn't look at him.

"Hey, freckles."

Jacob knew that voice too. It was a kid named Winter—the big catcher. He was as big as a full-grown man.

"We're going to beat you guys on Wednesday."

Jacob couldn't resist. "Just like you beat the Padres today?"

Winter didn't like that. He got up and came over close to Jacob. "Don't get smart, little kid."

Jacob watched Kenny take a warm-up pitch.

"The ump robbed us. That's why we lost," Winter said. "Jimmy hit a home run and the ump said it was foul."

"That's a very sad story," Jacob said.

Winter took one step closer. "You have a mouth, you know it, little kid? You're the one who always acts like you're some kind of baseball announcer, aren't you?"

Jacob had decided to say nothing more.

"Let me tell you something, baby boy," Winter said. "We know *exactly* how to beat you guys. We've got a *new strategy*—a *secret weapon*."

Kenny threw the first pitch of the game. The Mariners' batter took a called strike.

"How come you're not playing, anyway?"

Jacob pretended Winter wasn't there.

"I think he kicked you off the team for having too much space between your two front teeth," Winter said.

To the Reds this was a great joke.

They all cracked up.

Jacob didn't find it nearly so funny.

★ 2 ★

From the Bleachers

Kenny struck out the first batter. The second batter tried to bunt, but Kenny got to the ball quickly and threw him out.

And then the Mariners' best hitter, the second baseman, came up.

Three swings and he was gone too.

Kenny was looking good—moving the ball up and down, out and in. He was also using a change-up once in a while to keep the batters off balance. Jacob thought he had even thrown a curve for the third strike.

That was good, of course. But it didn't make Jacob feel any better.

And the Reds were only making things worse.

"Hey, little *rookie star*," they kept yelling at Kenny, "you stink! Maybe the Mariners can't hit you—but *we* can."

The local newspaper had printed an article saying that Kenny was already a star as a first-year player. The players on the other teams weren't letting him live it down.

As Kenny walked off the field Gerstein yelled, "Hey, little star, I hope the coach doesn't make you pitch against us. We could all be thrown in jail for child abuse."

The Reds' players all laughed.

Kenny looked up and smiled.

They didn't like that.

"That kid ain't half as good as he thinks he is," Winter said.

Jacob thought of a few things to say, but he kept his mouth shut.

But then he heard one of the Reds say, "What else can we call him?"

Gerstein glanced back at Jacob, and then he said, "Don't talk so loud."

After that the Reds leaned together. Jacob could hear them laughing, but he wasn't sure what they were talking about.

Coach Wilkens had made a few changes

in the lineup. Little Brian Waters, who had been playing well lately, was leading off.

The Mariners had their best pitcher on the mound—a chubby kid named Pat Sullivan.

He got off to a bad start.

Brian hit an easy tap to him, but Sullivan had trouble digging it out of his glove, and then he tried to hurry to beat Brian—who was *fast*.

Sullivan threw high, and Brian was not only safe, he went to second on the error.

After that Henry White singled and scored Brian, and Kenny came up with Henry at first.

"Hey, little *mama's boy*!" Winter yelled. "Do a good job so Mommy will be proud."

All the Reds were ready with the same kind of stuff. "Hey, little star, show your *mommy* what you can do."

"Don't let your *mom* down, Sandoval!"

What was this? Jacob wondered.

It was true that Mrs. Sandoval had a loud voice. While Kenny had been pitching, she and Kenny's dad had yelled to him a few times. But most parents did that. What did the Reds think they were doing?

Kenny seemed not to notice. He hammered a line drive to right field for a single.

Henry moved to third.

Bunson was up next.

And now the Reds really let loose.

"Hey, *Buns*," Winter yelled. *"FAT buns."*

"Hey, Buns, you waddle when you walk!"

"You better work off a few pounds, *Buns*."

Jacob was really confused now. Bunson was a good-sized guy, but he was not fat at all.

Bunson didn't understand either. He turned and looked at the Reds' players.

They liked that. They all started yelling again—and all of them were saying the same kinds of things.

"Buns! Buns! Buns!"

"Shut up!" Bunson yelled.

The umpire told him to step up to bat. And he did. But he took a hard swing at the first pitch and missed.

The Reds' players went nuts. They screamed more of their insults.

Bunson let an outside pitch go by, and then he stepped out of the box and looked at the Reds again. He had a bad temper, and Jacob could see he was about ready to come into the stands after those guys.

The Reds loved it. They kept yelling until the umpire walked to the fence and said, "All right, that's enough. You can cheer all you want, but that's enough name-calling."

"His name *is* Buns," Winter yelled. "Ask his mother."

"I said that's enough," the umpire said, and the boys did quiet down for the moment.

But the damage had been done.

Bunson's temper was raging. He swung hard again and missed.

The Reds howled.

And then, to add to the trouble, Bunson struck out on a called strike that he thought was inside.

He spun around and argued with the umpire, and then he threw down his bat and walked to the dugout.

The Reds chanted, *"Buns. Buns. Buns."*

Luckily Sterling Malone, one of the

Dodgers' best hitters, was up next. Before the Reds could say much about him, he swatted the first pitch all the way to the fence in left field.

Two more runs scored.

Jacob thought that would shut up the Reds.

But it didn't. They kept working on all the Dodgers' players, teasing them and calling them names.

And it did seem to bother some of the Dodgers.

The game turned out closer than it first appeared it might. The Dodgers got a lot of hits, but they couldn't come through when they needed to drive the runs in.

Kenny pitched the first two innings, which used up his allowed innings for the week. Then Eddie Boschi took over. Both did well, but the Dodgers made more errors than usual.

Eventually the Reds' players decided to leave.

But Winter couldn't resist coming over to say good-bye to Jacob.

"So, little number six, what's the deal?"

he said. "Are you hurt or something? Or did your mommy tell you that you shouldn't play with the big, *mean* boys?"

Jacob looked up. He told himself not to say anything, but he couldn't hold back. "She told me to be kind to boys who are a little . . . *slow* . . . like you."

"Oh, you're a cute one, aren't you? If you weren't a baby, I'd bust your head for you."

Winter took a step away, and then he looked back and said, "I hope you're play-ing on Wednesday. Because I want to see how cute you are when you're on your back in the dirt."

"In the dirt? What are you talking about? What makes you think you'll do any better against us than you did against the Padres?"

"Because we've got a new strategy. Haven't you noticed?"

"*Winter*. Shut up!" Gerstein yelled.

"Okay. Okay." But then he said to Jacob, "Just wait and see what happens."

He started to walk away again, but then he stopped for one last shot. "Number six, why *aren't* you playing. Is is really true that you flunked out of third grade?"

That one hit a little too close to home.

Jacob had liked being mad at the Reds. It had given him something else to think about. But now that they were leaving, he had to think about sitting in the stands and not playing.

For a while he had almost forgotten the most important thing: This was the worst day of his life—even though the Dodgers won, five to four.

But that was not the point. If he had played, it would have been ten to nothing. He was just sure of it.

Jacob's big day had finally come—and he had spent it in the bleachers.

BOX SCORE, GAME 14

San Lorenzo Mariners 4   Angel Park Dodgers 5

	ab	r	h	rbi		ab	r	h	rbi
Cast cf	3	0	1	0	Waters rf	3	1	1	0
Smagler 2b	4	0	1	1	White 3b	4	1	2	1
Amey lf	3	0	0	0	Sandoval p	4	1	2	0
Tomas ss	2	0	0	0	Bunson ss	3	0	0	0
Antonangeli c	2	1	2	0	Malone cf	2	0	1	2
Rodriguez 1b	2	1	0	0	Roper 1b	2	1	2	0
Sullivan p	2	1	0	0	Boschi lf	2	1	1	0
Cisco rf	1	1	0	0	Bacon c	2	0	1	2
St. Mary 3b	1	0	1	1	Reinhold 2b	2	0	0	0
Korman c	1	0	0	0	Sloan 1b	1	0	0	0
Perez 3b	1	0	0	0	Sandia 2b	1	0	1	0
Watson rf	1	0	0	0					
ttl	**23**	**4**	**5**	**2**		**26**	**5**	**11**	**5**

Mariners	0	2	0	2	0	0—4
Dodgers	3	0	2	0	0	X—5

A Rule Is a Rule

Jacob put a lot of time in on his schoolwork for the next few days. He had a good talk with his teacher and promised he would stop fooling around.

But now he had to talk his mom and dad into letting him play in the next game. Kenny and Harlan forced the issue when they came over to see if he could work out with them.

"Wait here," he told them. "I gotta go ask."

They waited in his bedroom while he went out to face his parents.

But his dad was still upset.

"Son, I know you love baseball," he told Jacob. "But you have to put first things first. Reading and writing and arithmetic. Not catching and throwing and . . . punting."

"Punting is football, Dad. You mean bunting."

"Whatever."

Dad was a history teacher. He never had played sports, or even watched them much.

"But Dad. I'm going to be a major-league player. So that stuff *is* important."

Dad took off his reading glasses and looked over at Mom, as if to say, "This is your area." Mom was a PE teacher. She *did* know about sports.

"You *might* make it to the majors, son," Mom said. "Maybe you have the talent; maybe you don't. But whether you make it in sports or not, you need to develop that good brain of yours."

Jacob knew that was right—even if he did think some of the stuff at school was boring.

"Okay, Mom," he said. "I'm going to work *really* hard in school from now on."

"I hope you mean that." She was using her firm voice; she sounded like a coach.

"But can I practice? And can I play on Wednesday?"

Dad and Mom looked at each other. "Well, I was going to have you miss a week, to make sure you caught up," Dad said.

"I *am* catching up. I've done almost everything already."

"That shows how easy it is when you make the effort."

"I know, Dad. But I'm doing it. And this week we're playing the Reds. I really want to play."

Jacob waited, holding his breath.

Dad looked at Mom again, and she nodded.

"Well, okay. But remember—"

"*All right!*" Jacob yelled, and he ran down the hallway to his room. "I get to play. I get to play."

Harlan was sitting on the floor by Jacob's bed. "*Great,*" he said. "Let's go practice."

Jacob thought for a moment, and then he said, "Not right now. I still have more schoolwork to do than I . . . told them."

"Then get it done," Kenny said.

Jacob nodded. "I'll meet you at the park in about an hour."

Jacob found plenty of time for baseball *and* school that week. He even found time to study the sports page—as always.

Life was okay again.

He was back on the team!

When he showed up on Wednesday afternoon, he checked with the coach to make sure his dad had called.

"Yup. He said you've been working. I'm glad to hear it."

Just then the plate umpire, a guy probably only in his early twenties, walked up. "Coach?"

Coach Wilkens looked around.

"Could I talk to you for a minute? With the other coach?"

Coach Wilkens walked to home plate, where the Reds' coach—a huge, potbellied man—was waiting.

Jacob decided to follow along and see what was going on.

"Mr. Corbett is concerned about some

things your players have been doing," the umpire said.

Coach Wilkens smiled and shook Corbett's hand. "What's the trouble?" he asked.

"Several things," the man said, in a voice that sounded like a bass drum. "For one thing, that pitcher of yours—the big kid—"

"Bunson?"

"Yeah. He balks."

"Balks?"

"That's right. He don't come to a full stop when he drops his hands. He quick-pitches."

"I . . . haven't noticed that. But I'll talk to him."

"You better do that. I've warned the umpire here, and he says he'll call him for it."

"Okay. Anything else?"

Jacob couldn't believe how friendly Coach Wilkens sounded.

Coach Corbett held out a little booklet and pointed to an open page. "This here is the official Little League rule book. On page seventeen it says, and I'm quoting." He took a deep breath and then read, " 'The Official Shoulder Patch must be *affixed* to the upper *left* sleeve of the uniform blouse.' "

"Yes. Our players all have those."

"Look again. Check your catcher."

Billy Bacon was warming up Rodney Bunson down the left field line. Coach Wilkens called to him, "Billy, come here."

Billy trotted over. "Yeah?" he said.

"Let me see your left shoulder."

Billy rotated the wrong way first, and the coach had to take hold of his shoulders and turn him back the other way.

Sure enough, the shoulder had no patch. "What happened to that Little League patch that was on here?"

"I don't know," Billy said. He stretched his neck to try to look at his own shoulder.

Coach Wilkens looked at the umpire. "I guess it came off. I'll pick one up tomorrow and get it sewn back on."

"That should be okay, I guess," the young umpire said, but he looked back at Coach Corbett.

"I'm sorry," the Reds' coach said. "But rules are rules, and the boys have to learn that. This boy does *not* have on an official uniform and can*not* be allowed to play."

"Well," the umpire said, "would it matter too much if I just warned him this time, and then—"

"If you're not going to enforce the rules, I'll call the Little League office. I'll tell them—"

"Wait a minute," Coach Wilkens said. "That's all right. I'll have Billy run home and see whether the patch is there some-where. Maybe he can get back to play part of the game."

The big coach nodded, as if to say, "Jus-tice has been done."

"Are there any other *infractions*?" Coach Wilkens asked. "I surely wouldn't want to take unfair advantage of you."

"Look, don't smart off to me. You're the ones breaking the rules. And now that you asked, yes, there is one more thing."

Jacob could see that Coach Wilkens was using all the control he had. He nodded and said, "All right. What is it?"

"It says right in the rule book that a player can't say anything that might *reflect* on the opposing team's players." He looked at the umpire. "That's like . . . make fun of 'em."

"Yes, I know that," the umpire said.

"Well, this team has a boy who acts like he's announcing the game—like one of them radio announcer fellows. But he says all sorts of abusive and insulting things about opposing players."

The umpire looked over at Coach Wilkens, who for the moment was just shaking his head.

Jacob couldn't believe it. Yeah, he liked to pretend he was announcing the game. But he didn't *abuse* anyone.

Coach Wilkens bit his words off carefully. "All right. I'll talk to Jacob. But Coach, you keep *your* kids quiet. They have the biggest mouths in this league."

"Now just a minute here. My boys—"

The umpire stepped in front of the big-bellied coach. "We'll have no name-calling or anything of that sort—from either side," the umpire said. "I'll see to that."

"Good," Coach Wilkens said, and he walked away.

Jacob still couldn't believe the Reds' coach could get away with something like that.

But Coach Wilkens said, "You heard him. No broadcasting today. Let's just keep our mouths shut and show them something with our *bats*."

★ 4 ★

Psyche Out

When the Dodgers heard what the Reds'
coach had complained about, they were mad.

Billy Bacon's mom drove Billy home. She
said the patch had been loose, so she pulled
it off before she washed the uniform, and
she forgot to sew it back on.

So that would only be a problem for an
inning or two. Harlan had been practicing
at catcher. He was due to try it in a game
sometime.

But maybe not such a big game.

Bunson said he would make sure he
stopped his hands when he brought them

down to pitch, and he was pretty sure he did that anyway.

Jacob said he'd be sure not to do his announcing.

"But the *Reds* better keep their mouths shut," Sterling Malone said.

"Look," the coach told all the players. "They're trying anything they can. What we can't do is let them get to us. No matter what they say, just play baseball."

But the Reds started in on Bunson as soon as he walked to the mound. Even one of the player's fathers stood by the fence and yelled, "Hey, pitcher, you lucked out last time! Next time you balk, you're out of here."

When Bunson delivered his first pitch, all the Reds screamed at once, *"Balk! Balk!"*

The umpire ignored them.

Jacob wondered how the Reds could be that stupid. A pitcher couldn't balk with no one on base.

But Bunson looked upset. He looked at the Reds' bench. "Oh, sure," he said.

His next pitch didn't have its usual snap.

Jimmy Gerstein was up, and he drove the ball past first base for a single.

Now Bunson was mad at himself. The Reds—and all their fans—were going crazy.

Jacob realized what was going on. The Reds knew about Bunson's temper. If they could get him mad, maybe he wouldn't pitch well.

So that was the secret "strategy."

Bunson got his sign from Harlan. He rocked and stretched, brought his hands down, and . . .

"Balk! Balk!" the Reds all screamed.

Bunson made an awkward pitch, well high, and then he spun and looked at the Reds' bench. "What are you talking about?" he said. But the Reds' players just laughed at him.

The umpire stepped out from behind the plate. "All right, boys. That's enough. There was no balk."

"Buns *did* balk!" Winter yelled out. "We saw him."

"I said that's enough."

Bunson pointed a finger at Winter and shook it, but he didn't say anything. He walked back to the mound. He threw hard and low.

The batter—the little second baseman—swung and missed.

Bunson was fired up.

Boom!

His pitch powered into Harlan's glove, and the batter didn't even swing.

Bunson got the ball back, took his sign, wound up, and let fly again.

The ball was a firecracker, low and hard again. The batter struck out swinging.

But Harlan missed the ball. It skittered under his glove and rolled all the way to the backstop. He hurried after it and threw to second, but Gerstein was able to beat the throw.

The batter was out, but now the Reds had a runner at second.

"Come on, Harlan," Bunson said.

"Yeah, come on, Harlan," the Reds all echoed.

"Don't get mad at him, *Buns*. He's just a little rookie."

The umpire gave the Reds' bench a long look, but he must have decided they weren't "abusive."

Not quite.

But Bunson was definitely upset.

Suddenly he couldn't throw strikes. He walked the left fielder on four pitches.

That meant Winter—the biggest mouth of all—was up to bat.

As he walked to the plate, he yelled, "Give me a fat one—just like your buns, *Buns!*"

Jacob saw Bunson take a quick step toward Winter and then stop himself.

The Reds all laughed.

The umpire didn't.

"All right. That's all. The next time I hear you call any names, of any sort, you're ejected from this game."

"But sir, that's his name."

Harlan spun around. "No it isn't. His name is Bunson."

Winter spoke very sincerely. "Oh, really? I always thought it was just 'Buns.'"

The Reds were cracking up.

Bunson was *burning*.

Bunson fired hard, but he forced the ball,

and it floated on him. Winter hammered it hard and long—and way back.

Over the left field fence!

Three runs scored.

Coach Wilkens gave the Reds time to celebrate, and then he walked to the mound. Jacob knew what he was telling Bunson: to ignore all the smart stuff.

Jacob just wasn't sure Bunson could do it.

But he did seem to calm down.

He got the next two batters on ground balls to finish out the inning, and then he walked from the mound—without even looking at the Reds.

When the players came running in, Jacob was a little surprised at how upset they were.

He soon found out why.

Danny Sandia was fuming. "When that Gerstein kid got to second, he said, 'What are you doing in the game, *bench warmer*?' I told him to shut his mouth."

Danny usually didn't start the games. Gerstein had known just the right thing to get his goat.

"Hey, you should have heard what he said

to me when he was on first," Jenny Roper told them "'Hey, Roper,' he said, 'you're pretty good for a *girl*.'"

"They were talking to me too," Harlan said.

He didn't sound as mad as the others. He sat with his elbows on his knees, looking at the ground.

"What did they say to you?" Jacob asked him.

"Just the usual stuff. That I was a rookie and I didn't know how to catch. And—well—about my ears."

"*Ears?*"

"Yeah."

"What did they say about your ears?"

"That they're big. Which is true."

Coach Wilkens had started out to the coach's box, but he stepped back. "All right, now listen," he said. "You can see what they're trying to do to you. Just ignore all that stuff."

"Why don't you complain to the umpire, the way their coach did?" Henry White asked.

"We can complain all we want, but when they're outside his hearing range, there's not one thing he can do."

"But it's not fair."

"Let's not get into all that, Henry. These kids think they can beat us if they can get us mad. They've watched us get ourselves in trouble that way before. Let's not let them get away with it today."

"Yeah, well, maybe we've got a few things we can say to *them*," Danny said.

"*No!*" Coach Wilkens pointed a finger at Danny. "I won't have it. We'll play *baseball,* not word games. And we won't bad-mouth anybody. Do you all hear that?"

No one said anything, but everyone nodded, and then Henry said, "Come on. Let's go out there and blast them with our bats."

It was a great idea.

But Henry couldn't quite do it. He led off, and swung too hard. He popped the ball up.

And Danny swung *way* too hard. He struck out.

Kenny was calmer than the others. He

kept his head and took a nice stroke, but he hit a looper right to the shortstop.

The Dodgers were out, in order—just like that—and they were looking very frustrated.

★ 5 ★

Seeing Red

Bunson struggled, but he kept his control. The Reds weren't yelling as much now that the umpire had warned them.

Billy also got back and took over the catching in the third inning. That helped too. But Billy was *mad.*

So were some of the other Dodgers.

Danny Sandia was the worst. In the third inning he let a ground ball get by him. The runner—the little second baseman—teased him about his error, and Danny tried not to let that bother him.

He fielded the next ball and only had to flip it to first, but he fired too hard and threw it over Jenny's head.

Bunson got tough and made Winter roll into a force at third. But then the center fielder grounded a ball toward Kenny.

Kenny went to his left, grabbed the ball, and was about to make the short throw for the force at second. But Danny had forgotten to cover second.

Kenny spun and threw to first, but too late.

Another run scored.

Danny stomped on the ground.

One of the Reds yelled, "Hey, Sandia, the game's called *baseball*! It's a little different than *benchwarming*!"

Danny lost it. "Shut your mouth! Do you hear me?" he screamed.

Coach Wilkens took Danny out of the game.

All the Reds got was another warning.

And things didn't go much better on offense, even though it seemed for a time they would. Kenny and Bunson got back-to-back singles in the fourth inning, and Brian Waters drove them both in with a double.

Jenny followed with a single, and Eddie walked. The go-ahead run was on base. The Dodgers had their chance.

Billy could hardly wait to get into the batter's box.

But Jacob saw Winter step up close to him and say something, and Billy spun around. Billy was half Winter's size, but he was ready to fight right then and there.

The umpire and Coach Wilkens stopped all that. But Billy was messed up. The pitcher didn't get a single pitch in the strike zone, but Billy swung three times and struck out.

The rally was over, and the Reds were still ahead, 4 to 2.

When Billy came back to get his catcher's equipment, he was mad enough to take a bite out of the chain-link fence.

Everyone wanted to know what Winter had said, but Billy wouldn't tell them.

And he was not the only one who was upset. Little Brian Waters had had a good game, but he was steaming about all the Reds' comments about his size.

Henry was fed up too. Winter had said to him, "I thought you were supposed to be a good hitter. I guess that was a joke?"

The Reds had come up with a name for, or something to say to, everyone on the team. They just didn't let the umpire hear them.

After the fourth inning, Jacob went in to play center field for Sterling Malone. Sterling was as upset as anyone. He had struck out twice.

Jacob stood in the outfield and tried to keep himself calm. He did his broadcast, far away, where no one could hear him.

"That's right, fans, the mighty Dodgers are behind by two runs. But don't give up. These kids can come back."

"I'll tell you what I think, Frank," Jacob said to himself, in his cowboy-style voice. "I think Jacob Scott is going to *whack* his first Little League homer—and save the day for the Dodgers."

"Well, now, let's not get carried away, Hank. Scott is not a power hitter. I think a timely single would do just as well."

"Yeah, maybe. But that boy looks calm and collected to me. I think he's going to do something *big*."

And on he went. He could say it all out there in center and not get in trouble.

But his announcing didn't change what happened.

The Reds went on to score two in the top of the fifth, partly because of an error by Jeff Reinhold.

Kenny doubled in the bottom of the fifth to drive in Henry White. That got one of the runs back. But when the Dodgers came up in the bottom of the sixth, they were down by three runs.

Jacob had gotten his chance in the fifth. He came close when he hit a line drive, barely foul, with Kenny on second. And he did manage a walk. But he and Kenny ended up stranded on base when the inning ended.

So it all came down to the last inning. At least Eddie Boschi started things right with a solid single.

"Hank," Jacob announced in the dugout, "I think the pitcher is losing a little off his fastball."

"That's *right*!" Bunson yelled. "He's losing it. Let's make those guys *pay* for all the stuff they've been saying."

Billy Bacon was walking toward the batter's box. He turned around and said, "Watch this."

They watched. And they yelled.

But Billy hit a grounder that wouldn't

have bruised a baby's bottom. Eddie ran hard, slid hard, but he was forced at second.

"Don't give up on the Dodgers yet," Jacob announced. "Henry White is coming up. My hunch is, he'll keep this thing going."

Jacob was mostly just talking to himself, but that was all right. He needed the calming effect—and the confidence.

And Frank's hunch—or Jacob's—was right.

Henry stung a fastball into the left-center gap. It went for a double, and Billy scored all the way from first.

But the Dodgers were still down by two. They needed to get people on base and keep the rally going.

Jeff Reinhold was coming up. He looked mad. But he hit an easy fly to short center field. Henry had to hold at second.

"Don't give up," Jacob said in Frank's voice. "Sandoval is coming up. He could tie this thing up with one swing."

Kenny walked to the plate and took a hard practice swing.

And then he surprised everyone.

He put down a perfect bunt. Winter went after the ball, but he had no chance to get Kenny.

The tying runs were now on base. Kenny had set the table for Bunson.

"Don't go away," Jacob said. "The Dodgers' star is coming up to bat with a chance to pull this game out of the fire."

The team cheered, but Jacob was nervous. He was now on deck. He hoped that Bunson could end the game with a homer.

But the Reds' coach wobbled out to the mound and had a talk with the pitcher.

Jacob knew what was coming. The Reds gave Bunson an intentional walk. They figured they would take their chances with Jacob—the little rookie.

"Well, fans," Jacob said as he walked to the plate, "the Reds have made a mistake this time. They've put the winning run on base. Scott can be very tough when he has to be. He can—"

"He can't do that!" Winter was yelling. "That's the kid my coach was talking about. He acts like he's announcing the game."

"You'll have to stop that," the umpire said.

Jacob had hardly realized what he was doing. But it was hard for him to stop. He needed to tell himself he could do it.

He tried to talk under his breath, but it wasn't the same.

The first pitch was down the middle. Jacob didn't swing. He was suddenly hoping for a walk.

He stepped out of the box and talked to himself—inside his head. "Yes, Hank, the boy looks confident. He shouldn't have any trouble with this pitcher."

He stepped back in, got ready, and this time he swung.

Foul ball.

He had barely ticked it.

And he had swung badly. He felt as awkward as he had in the very first games of the season. What was going on?

"Frank," he said out loud, "I wouldn't let that oh-and-two count fool you. This boy can—"

"He's doing it again," Winter said.

And Jacob shut up.

He stepped back to the plate, and he told himself that he would stroke the ball for a big hit.

The pitch was high, but Jacob started his swing. And then he tried to hold up.

He thought maybe he had.

But he heard the umpire bellow, *"Steee-rike three!"*

Jacob sank right to the ground.

He had let the whole team down.

How could the Dodgers lose to the *Reds*?

He had been wrong about watching the game from the bleachers. That wasn't the worst thing in the world.

This was. Losing the game for the whole team.

Jacob wanted to dig a hole under home plate, climb in, and die.

BOX SCORE, GAME 15

Cactus Hills Reds 6   Angel Park Dodgers 4

	ab	r	h	rbi		ab	r	h	rbi
Gerstein 3b	4	1	1	0	White 3b	4	1	2	1
Alfonsi 2b	1	1	0	0	Sandia 2b	1	0	0	0
Schulman lf	2	1	1	0	Sandoval ss	4	1	3	1
Winter c	4	2	1	3	Bunson p	3	1	2	0
Mendelsohn cf	4	0	1	1	Malone cf	2	0	0	0
Tovar p	3	1	1	0	Waters rf	2	0	1	2
Lum 1b	1	0	0	0	Roper 1b	3	0	1	0
Bonthuis rf	3	0	0	0	Boschi lf	2	0	1	0
Young ss	1	0	0	0	Sloan c	1	0	0	0
Rutter rf	2	0	2	1	Bacon c	2	1	0	0
Higdon 2b	2	0	0	0	Reinhold 2b	3	0	0	0
Trulis cf	0	0	0	0	Scott cf	1	0	0	0
ttl	**27**	**6**	**7**	**5**		**28**	**4**	**10**	**4**

Reds	3	0	1	0	2	0—6
Dodgers	0	0	0	2	1	1—4

★ 6 ★

Are We Having Fun?

The coach was standing up, with his hands on his hips. The Dodgers were all sitting down, looking at the grass.

"You look like you're at a funeral," Coach Wilkens said.

We are, Jacob told himself. *MINE.*

He knew he could never be happy again. The Dodgers had lost to the pukey, sickening Reds—and it was all his fault.

That was as low as life could get.

But the coach was saying, "We can't win every game, kids. Some days we're going to get outplayed."

"They didn't out*play* us," Sterling said. "They *cheated.*"

"If you're saying they're bad sports, I agree. But you didn't have to let that stuff bother you."

"It's *hard* when they call you names," Billy said.

"What did they call you, Billy?" Coach Wilkens asked. He smiled a little.

Billy hesitated, and then barely whispered, "Piggly Wiggly."

"What?"

Jacob heard a couple of guys snicker.

"Winter said to me, 'Hey, Bacon, you're named right. You look like a pig.' Then he started calling me Piggly Wiggly."

When Coach Wilkens laughed, everyone did.

Except for Billy.

And Jacob.

And then even Billy laughed. "If I'm a pig, he's a *big hog*," he said.

The mood got a lot better. Everyone followed the coach to his van for cold drinks.

Everyone except Jacob. He sat on the grass cross-legged, his chin propped on his hands. He didn't think he could ever laugh again. In fact, he was trying hard not to cry.

He kept seeing it all over again: him up

to bat with a chance to be a hero, and then swinging the bat like a *baby*.

He was still sitting there when the coach came walking back to him. "Are you okay, Jacob?" he asked.

Jacob sort of shrugged. He didn't look up.

"Jacob, everybody made outs. You just made the last one."

"I could have won the game for us."

The coach sat on the grass. He patted Jacob on the knee. "Look, I know how you feel. But another day you'll get the big hit. It's not that big a thing. If you take the game so seriously that it isn't fun, why play?"

Jacob didn't say anything for a time. He was thinking. But then he said, "I want to make it to the majors."

"Hey, the biggest stars in the major leagues only get a hit about three times out of every ten."

That was true. Jacob knew that.

"I'll tell you something else. In the long run, that good mind of yours is more important than your athletic ability. That's why I was hard on you when you slacked off in school."

"Don't you think I can make it in baseball?"

"I don't know. But I don't think you ought to feel sorry for yourself. You're good at sports and you're also very smart. Not many kids have that much going for them."

That made sense too. Jacob was already feeling better than he thought he ever would again.

"You know, one of the best things you've done for this team is your radio announcing. That's fun. It keeps the kids loose."

Jacob looked up. He was surprised. "Really?"

"Sure. Now listen. I don't want you to get down on yourself. I need you to keep us having fun. Can you do that?"

"I guess so."

"Look at it this way. No one called you Piggly Wiggly."

And Jacob did what he hadn't thought he would ever do again.

He laughed.

But Jacob took the coach seriously. He liked the idea that he could use his brain to do something to help the team.

He even went to the library and did some reading on sports psychology. By the time Saturday came around, Jacob had a plan.

On Friday he talked to the players at school. He asked them to be at the game half an hour early.

On Saturday morning, as the kids started showing up, he had them gather beneath the shade of some eucalyptus trees.

Once everyone was there, he had them lie back and relax. Then he punched the button on his tape player, and soft violin music began to play.

Bunson sat up. "What's that junk?" he asked.

"It's restful music," Jacob said. "I want you to listen to it and let yourself relax. Completely relax."

"You gotta be kidding," Jeff said. "I'm not doing that."

"Come on. The coach told us we had to relax and play our best. This will help. I read about it in a book."

"No way," Jeff told him, and he stood up. Bunson and Danny were getting up too.

"Hey, it's worth a try," Henry said.

Everyone listened to Henry. He wasn't a

rookie, and he was someone all the kids respected.

All the same Bunson said, "It's stupid."

"Maybe. Maybe not," Henry said. "But Jacob's smart. If he read something that might help us—what can it hurt to try it?"

Jeff complained, and so did Danny. But Bunson said, "What the heck? I can use some rest."

So they all lay down again.

"Now listen to the music," Jacob said. "Let it lift you."

"It sounds like that 'easy listening' crap some of those FM stations play," Jeff said.

A lot of the kids laughed.

"Now, come on. Don't do that," Jacob said. "Let yourself float." He made his voice mellow and low. "Think of floating on a cloud. Breathe deep. Let the air out. Breathe deep."

"Sounds like those exercise women on TV," Bunson said, and everyone laughed again.

Jacob ignored that one. "Feel that cloud lift you," he said. "Breathe deep."

But now someone was making snoring noises.

Jacob wasn't going to give up. "Now, picture this. The Padres' pitcher is winding up. You're breathing easy. You know you can hit the ball."

Jacob let the music play for a while. "Yes," he kept saying. "You *know* you can hit the ball."

"That's because the Padres' pitcher stinks," Sterling said.

"No, no. Think of it the other way. You see the ball, big and round and white. It floats before your eyes, and you time your swing—perfectly."

"*All right!*" Bunson barked. "That's right. We all hit today. Let's go get 'em."

"No, no. Not yet," Jacob yelled. Everyone was jumping up. "We've got lots of time."

"Okay. So we're relaxed now," Sterling said.

"Not really. You never really got into it. I want to try one more thing."

"Come on, Jacob."

But Henry came to the rescue again. "I like this," he said. "I think it's helping me. Go ahead, Jacob."

"All right. Everyone get comfortable,"

Jacob said. "I want you to visualize yourself doing well. But you need to drift almost into a trance. Let me try one other thing."

Jacob let them listen to the music. Then he announced, "I'll now read 'The Daffodils,' by William Wordsworth. Listen and relax. Try to envision the peaceful scene."

He began to read:

"I wandered lonely as a cloud
That floats on high o'er vales and hills,
When all at once I saw a crowd,
A host of golden daffodils;
Beside the lake, beneath—"

But that's when Bunson said, "Oh, puke. Give me a break, Jacob. I'm not going to listen to *flower poems*."

And that was the end of Jacob's great plan to relax the Dodgers.

Everyone got up and followed Bunson to the playing field.

Henry told Jacob he still thought it was a good idea, but he left too.

Only Kenny and Harlan stayed with

Jacob. "I liked that," Kenny said. "I feel good. I think I'm going to hit well today."

"Yeah, but you *always* do."

"Maybe the poem was going a little too far," Harlan said. "You know Bunson."

"Yeah, I sure do," Jacob said. He was already feeling down again. Maybe he couldn't help the team either way—with his bat *or* his brain.

★ **7** ★

Backfire

Jacob and Kenny and Harlan had just started walking toward the playing field when they heard the argument break out.

They heard Bunson yell, "You call me that again, kid, and I'm going to spread your nose all over your face."

"Oh, oh. It's the Reds," Kenny said, and the rookies ran toward the mob of players in red and blue uniforms.

Jacob knew what had happened. The Reds had just finished their game and were leaving. They must have started the name-calling again.

By the time Jacob got to the trouble, a couple of dads had gotten in between the two teams. The Reds were now walking away, but some of them were still looking back, yelling.

"Have a good game, *Buns*!" Gerstein shouted.

The Reds' center fielder turned clear around and said, "Would someone give a little *slop* to Piggly Wiggly? He needs to grow."

Henry grabbed Billy to keep him from running after the kid.

"Calm down, Billy," Danny said. "Jacob can read you another flower poem."

"Shut up, Danny," Henry said.

"Oh, that's right. I'm sorry. Henry *likes* the little *flower* poems and the *pretty* music."

"Yeah, maybe I do. Do you want to make something of it?"

He stepped toward Danny.

Jacob saw Coach Wilkens running toward the group, but Danny stepped nose to nose with Henry. "Yeah, if *you* want to," he growled.

"Hey!" the coach yelled. "What's going on?"

Bunson took it on himself to tell the story.

"Those stupid Reds started calling us names again and—"

"I'm talking about Danny and Henry," Coach Wilkens said.

"That's *Jacob's* fault. He got a big idea to play this sissy music and read poems to us. It was stupid."

"What does that have to do with . . . this?" He pointed to the boys again.

Suddenly everyone was talking. Danny and Bunson and Jeff told the coach—all at the same time—about Jacob's stupid plan. And Henry and Jacob went on the defense.

"Wait a minute. *STOP!*" the coach yelled.

Once everyone was quiet, he said, "I can't believe this. I've talked to you all week about keeping your cool with the other teams, and now here you are ready to kill *each other*."

Jacob could see how disgusted he was.

"Now get out there and warm up, and forget this whole thing," he finally said.

But no one moved for the moment.

"Go on. Get going. Remember—we're going to have *fun!*"

But Coach Wilkens didn't sound very fun himself.

The team walked out to the field.

They looked like a bunch of prisoners on a chain gang.

Fun?

Jacob couldn't believe it. Maybe he should quit the team, so they would have a chance.

His only hope was that the steam had been let off now. Maybe once they scored some runs, they would feel better.

But no such luck.

When Henry White went out to bat, Bunson yelled, "Think of *flowers,* Henry! Knock the petals off that big *daffodil!*"

Henry looked back at Bunson. "You better lay off," he said.

The coach told Bunson to quiet down.

Bunson did.

But Henry grounded out.

And Jenny made a bad swing. She squibbed a grounder off the end of her bat, and she was thrown out by the catcher.

Kenny was the only one who looked natural—and confident. He stroked the ball past the pitcher and into center field.

Bunson marched up to the plate. He was mad enough to eat the thing.

He *pounded* the first pitch. But he got under the ball and lifted it very high. It was just a long out.

"Come on," Billy yelled at everybody. "We *erased* this pitcher last time. He's got nothing."

Billy went out to take some warm-up throws from Eddie Boschi, who was pitching.

And Eddie looked pretty good. His motion was right. But he looked grim, maybe worried. He tried to be too careful with the first batter—Roberts, the quick second baseman.

On a three-and-one count he came down the middle with the pitch. Roberts powered the ball over Brian's head in right field.

Roberts stretched the hit into a triple when Brian's throw was off-line to the cutoff man.

"Come on, Eddie," Bunson yelled from the outfield. "You can get *these* guys out." He wasn't calming down at all.

Eddie tried.

But the right fielder got lucky on an outside pitch. He swung late and flared the ball toward right. Jeff chased it, but it dropped just beyond his glove.

Roberts was heading home.

Jeff didn't have a chance, but he threw anyway. All that did was give the runner a chance to go to second.

"What are you doing, Jeff?" Henry yelled.

Jacob was watching all this from the bench. He just shook his head.

The team was forgetting everything the coach had told them. They were getting uptight, pressuring themselves, blaming each other, making mental mistakes. They had been better off when they were mad at the Reds.

Eddie made a good pitch and got the Padres' shortstop to pop up. But the next batter, the first baseman, waited on Eddie's change-up, and he knocked a long fly to left.

Bunson was one guy who almost never made a mistake in the field. But the ball stayed up. Bunson misjudged it. Suddenly he had to leap, and the ball glanced off his glove and rolled to the fence.

Sterling chased the ball down and fired it back to the infield. But another run scored on the "luck-out" double.

Henry kicked at the bag at third, and then he looked out at Bunson. He didn't say a word, but Bunson knew what he was thinking. "Shut up, Henry!" he yelled.

The Padres saw what was happening to the Dodgers, and they started to pour it on.

"Hey, Bunson, don't blame it on Henry!" the runner at second yelled. "You're the one who couldn't catch the ball."

Bunson pointed at the kid. "*You* shut up too," he said.

Both Coach Wilkens and the second-base umpire yelled to him to quiet down. The runner got the same warning.

Things were bad, but Jacob could see disaster coming.

Big Jim Cegielski, the catcher, was coming up. He was the power hitter on the Padres' team. And the Dodgers were acting as if they all hated each other.

Jacob wondered who would make the next big mistake.

It didn't take long to find out.

Eddie tried too hard to make a big pitch. He fell back into his old habit of throwing with his arm and not with his whole body.

Cegielski *pulverized* it.

Jacob knew it was gone. He only glanced up to see the umpire signal "home run," and then he ducked his head again so he wouldn't have to watch Cegielski circle the bases.

Four to nothing.

The Padres weren't *that* good. How could this be happening? The whole season was going down the drain—not with a gurgle but a *whoosh*.

Coach Wilkens walked out and had a talk with Eddie.

He did look better on the next pitch. And he ended up getting the next two batters to get out of the inning.

But the damage had been done.

The Dodgers were in a bad state when they came running to the dugout.

"I can't believe this!" Billy said, and he kicked the fence. "How can we lose to the stupid Padres?"

"Who said we're losing?" Sterling yelled. "Let's get some *runs*."

But he sounded mad, not sure of himself.

Jacob looked around. One thing was sure: no one was having any fun. Not even Coach Wilkens.

★ 8 ★

Time to Play

====================

Things kept going the same way for a couple of innings. The Padres didn't score—although they threatened to in both innings.

But the Dodgers didn't even threaten.

Then, in the fourth, Jeff booted a ground ball and Eddie walked a guy. Cegielski made the Dodgers pay for their mistakes again. He hit a two-run double.

The Dodgers were in a whole lot of trouble. When they came to bat in the top of the fourth, they were four runs behind.

Something big had to happen to turn things around.

Jacob was trying hard to think what he

could do. He still felt that he had caused the problems the team was having today.

At least one player—Kenny, again—was still himself. He started the inning with a long shot into the right field corner. He went all the way to third for a stand-up triple.

Maybe it was time to try the broadcast. The coach had said that helped the players stay loose.

"That may be the spark the Dodgers have been needing," Jacob said in his deep announcer's voice.

"Yes, Hank, I feel the same way. The young man coming up, *Burner* Bunson, just could be the one to start the *fire*."

Okay, so it wasn't very funny.

But Jeff didn't have to groan.

And Danny didn't have to tell him to shut up.

"Bunson is stepping in, fans. He's got a dog-determined look on his face. He looks downright . . . oh, wait a minute. That's the catcher I was looking at. That kid is *uuugly*."

This actually got a bit of a laugh.

From Billy.

But Bunson swung and missed.

Sterling shook his head as if to say, "Nothing is going to go right today."

Jacob had to think fast. "If I had a kid that ugly on my team, I'd paint a face on his butt and make him walk around backward."

Billy liked that one. In fact, several of the kids laughed.

Jacob was breaking a little ice.

But just then Kenny, of all people, made a silly mistake.

Bunson hit a hard shot on the ground to the right side. Kenny broke for the plate. But the second baseman made the stop, and Cegielski screamed, "Home!"

The second baseman turned and fired the ball to Cegielski.

"Oh, *no!*" Sterling yelled.

Jacob ducked his head.

Another disaster.

But when he looked up, Kenny had thrown on the brakes, and he was heading back to third. Cegielski ran after him, and then he threw to the third baseman.

Kenny stopped again. He was in a rundown.

Jacob saw Bunson use the chance to move on to second. That was one good thing.

But Danny shouted, "What was Kenny *thinking*?"

Kenny trotted carefully toward home, looking back, and then, when the throw came, he reversed himself and got chased back toward third. He was barely able to avoid the tag as Cegielski tossed back to the shortstop, covering third this time.

But no one was covering home!

Cegielski's momentum had taken him out of the play, and no one had backed him up.

Kenny had a chance.

The shortstop chased after him, and the pitcher was charging toward the plate.

At the last second the shortstop tossed the ball home.

Kenny slid as the ball popped into the pitcher's glove . . . and back out.

"*SAFE!*" the umpire called.

The Dodgers roared.

But Cegielski was running toward the plate. He was crazy mad, but not at the umpire. "Tony, what were you doing?" he yelled at the pitcher. "Why didn't you cover home?"

The pitcher turned and walked away.

Cegielski threw his mask on the ground and walked toward the mound. "What were you doing?" he yelled.

The pitcher spun around. "I thought he was going to be out at third!" he shouted. He pulled off his hat and rubbed his arm over his sweaty black hair. His face was bright red.

"Wait a minute, fans," Jacob announced. "We have a rhubarb going on here. But only one team is in on it. Are the Padres really mad at . . . *the Padres*? Is the catcher going to punch out his own pitcher?"

"Punch him, Cegielski!" Jeff yelled, and the Dodgers all laughed.

But Cegielski was still steaming. "You know you're supposed to come home and cover. How many times have we worked on that?"

The Padres' coach was walking to the mound, saying, "Boys. Boys. Come on. Let's stop this."

But just then the shortstop yelled, "Get

off his back, Jim! You should have had him the first time. You threw too soon."

"No way!" Cegielski yelled back at him.

"Oh, fans, I hate to see this," Jacob announced. "These young men are actually attacking each other with . . . cruel, unfeeling words. I just can't believe how *heartless* they're being."

The Dodgers were having fun now. They loved watching the Padres scream at each other.

And Jacob was cracking them up.

The Padres' coach was yelling at the boys to get back to their positions and to shut their mouths. He was starting to lose his temper too.

"I think the coach is considering a good spanking for all three of these very bad boys," Jacob said.

"That's right, Frank," the cowboy announcer said. "I don't blame him. This is a dark night in the history of baseball. I've never—anywhere—seen players, all on the same team, *abuse* each other."

Suddenly the Dodger players weren't laughing quite so much.

"Yes, Hank, that's a good point. There's really no excuse for this. I'm sure you'd have to search far and wide to find another example of players yelling at members of their *own* team this way. To find such *complete idiots* who would actually—"

"Okay, okay," Bunson said. "We get the point."

"Yeah," Jenny said. "Let's not act like those blockheads. Let's play *baseball.*"

"Do I have to play with that stupid Danny?" Henry said, and he laughed.

"Yeah, as long as I have to play with that idiot Henry."

The coach walked over to the dugout when he heard the laughter.

"Do you see now how stupid that looks?" He pointed out at the Padres.

The Dodger players were nodding.

"Well, then, let's lay off that stuff. Let's play together and have some fun. Let's score some *runs!*"

All the Dodgers yelled, *"Yeah!"*

That was the beginning.

Malone slapped a single into left field— and made it look easy.

Bunson scored.

Eddie followed with another single. Jeff was careful not to swing at anything bad, and he ended up walking.

Brian came up with the bases loaded and stroked the ball right up the middle.

Two more runs scored.

The rally had just begun.

The Padres started making errors, and the Dodgers could do nothing wrong. When the dust had finally settled, ten runs were across in the inning.

And before the game was over, the Dodgers had scored sixteen times.

The poor Padres were yelling at each other, blaming, making mistakes.

The Dodgers were laughing and having fun.

And Jacob got in the act when he lined a single to center and drove in Kenny, and then scored on a hit by old "Piggly Wiggly."

Once the win was beyond doubt, Jacob looked for the book bag he had brought with him. He got out his geography book and started reading.

Kenny was the first one to spot him.

"What are you doing?" he said, and laughed.

Jacob had been waiting for someone to ask. "Oh. Well, you know—baseball is something I do for fun. I'm really more the brainy type."

"Yeah, right."

Other players were listening now.

"Oh, sure," Jacob said. "I knew we'd have no trouble with the Padres—not after I got everyone relaxed with my pretty music and my nice poetry. So I brought something along to keep myself entertained. There's nothing quite like geography for a good time."

Everyone was laughing.

And Jacob enjoyed that.

The truth was, though, he had brought the book because he still had some catching up to do. And he really hadn't thought the game would be close.

But he was glad he had done it when the coach spotted him and gave him a big thumbs-up.

And Kenny said, "Well, it's about time you got 'em together."

"Got what together?" Jacob asked.

"Your brains and your . . . bat."

Jacob liked that. He gave Kenny one of his big, gap-toothed grins. And then he settled back and really did read some geography. The stuff was kind of interesting, once a guy put his mind to it: Asia . . . what an amazing continent!

Still, he hoped he would get up again. He wanted to *smash* one more base hit today. And he wanted to keep hitting all season. The team was back in the running for the championship!

BOX SCORE, GAME 16

Angel Park Dodgers 16

	ab	r	h	rbi
White 3b	4	2	2	1
Roper 1b	3	1	1	1
Sandoval ss	5	3	4	1
Bunson lf	4	2	3	2
Malone cf	4	1	2	1
Boschi p	5	1	1	0
Reinhold 2b	2	1	1	1
Waters rf	3	1	2	2
Bacon c	4	1	2	4
Sandia ss	0	1	0	0
Sloan 1b	1	1	0	0
Scott rf	1	1	1	1
ttl	**36**	**16**	**19**	**14**

Santa Rita Padres 6

	ab	r	h	rbi
Roberts 2b	4	1	3	0
Brenchley rf	2	2	1	1
Jorgensen ss	3	1	1	0
Durkin 1b	4	1	1	1
Cegielski c	3	1	3	4
Blough 3b	2	0	0	0
Valenciano p	3	0	0	0
Brown lf	2	0	0	0
Shimer cf	2	0	0	0
Nakatani lf	1	0	0	0
Orosco cf	1	0	0	0
Kim p	1	0	0	0
	28	**6**	**9**	**6**

Dodgers	0	0	0	10	6	0—16
Padres	4	0	0	2	0	0—6

League standings after six games:
(Second half of season)

Giants	5–1
Dodgers	4–2
Reds	4–2
Mariners	3–3
A's	1–5
Padres	1–5

Fourth game scores:

Dodgers	5	Mariners	4
Giants	16	A's	1
Padres	4	Reds	3

Fifth game scores:

Reds	6	Dodgers	4
Giants	16	Padres	2
Mariners	8	A's	6

Sixth game scores:

Dodgers	16	Padres	6
Giants	17	Mariners	9
Reds	5	A's	3

DEAN HUGHES has written many books for children including the popular *Nutty* stories and *Jelly's Circus*. He has also published such works of literary fiction for young adults as the highly acclaimed *Family Pose*. When he's not attending Little League games, Mr. Hughes devotes his full time to writing. He lives in Utah with his wife and family.

ENTER THE ANGEL PARK ALL-STARS SWEEPSTAKES!

- The Grand Prize: a trip for four to the 1991 All-Star Game in Toronto
- 25 First Prizes: Louisville Slugger Little League bat personalized with the winner's name and the Angel Park All-Stars logo

See official entry rules below.

OFFICIAL RULES—NO PURCHASE NECESSARY

1. On an official entry form print your name, address, zip code, age, and the answer to the following question: What are the names of the three main characters in the Angel Park All-Stars books? The information needed to answer this question can be found in any of the Angel Park All-Stars books, or you may obtain an entry form, a set of rules, and the answer to the question by writing to: Angel Park Request, P.O. Box 3352, Syosset, NY 11775–3352. Each request must be mailed separately and must be received by November 1, 1990.

2. Enter as often as you wish, but each entry must be mailed separately to: ANGEL PARK ALL-STARS SWEEPSTAKES, P.O. Box 3335, Syosset, NY 11775–3335. No mechanically reproduced entries will be accepted. All entries must be received by December 1, 1990.

3. **Winners will be selected, from among correct entries received, in a random drawing conducted by National Judging Institute, Inc., an independent judging organization whose decisions are final on all matters relating to this sweepstakes. All prizes will be awarded and winners notified by mail. Prizes are nontransferable, and no substitutions or cash equivalents are allowed. Taxes, if any, are the responsibility of the individual winners. Winners may be asked to verify address or execute an affidavit of eligibility and release. No responsibility is assumed for lost, misdirected, or late entries or mail. Grand Prize consists of a three-day/two-night trip for a family of four to the 1991 All-Star Game in Toronto, Canada, including round-trip air transportation, hotel accommodations, game tickets, hotel-to-airport and hotel-to-game transfers, and breakfasts and dinners. In the event the trip is won by a minor, it will be awarded in the name of a parent or legal guardian. Trip must be taken on date specified or the prize will be forfeited and an alternate winner selected. RANDOM HOUSE, INC., and its affiliates reserve the right to use the prize winners' names and likenesses in any promotional activities relating to this sweepstakes without further compensation to the winners.**

4. Sweepstakes open to residents of the U.S. and Canada, except for the Province of Quebec. Employees and their families of RANDOM HOUSE, INC., and its affiliates, subsidiaries, advertising agencies, and retailers, and Don Jagoda Associates, Inc., may not enter. This offer is void wherever prohibited, and subject to all federal, state, and local laws.

5. **For a list of winners, send a stamped, self-addressed envelope to: ANGEL PARK WINNERS, P.O. Box 3347, Syosset, NY 11775–3347.**

Angel Park All-Stars Sweepstakes Official Entry Form

Name:_____ Age: _____

(Please Print)

Address_____

City/State/Zip:_____

What are the names of the three main characters in the Angel Park All-Stars books?

_____